Solomon's Tree

For Tsimpshian master-carver Victor Reece, his wife, writer Sharon Jinkerson, and their son, Solomon.

Our grateful thanks for your contributions to bridging our cultures. May the bridge grow stronger and wider so more people can dance across.

AS & JW

National Library of Canada Cataloguing in Publication Data
Spalding, Andrea.

Solomon's tree

ISBN 1-55143-217-X

I. Wilson, Janet, 1952- II. Title.

E99.T8S62 2002 j731'.75'0899741 C2002-910422-X

First published in the United States, 2002

Library of Congress Control Number: 2002104082

Summary: A boy is devastated when his beloved maple falls in a storm, and the transformational experience of making a Tsimpshian mask helps him deal with his grief.

Orca Book Publishers gratefully acknowledges the support for its publishing programs provided by the following agencies: the Government of Canada through the Book Publishing Industry Development Program (BPIDP), the Canada Council for the Arts, and the British Columbia Arts Council.

Teacher's guide available from Orca Book Publishers.

Design: Christine Toller
Printed and bound in Hong Kong

IN CANADA:
Orca Book Publishers
PO Box 5626, Station B
Victoria, BC Canada
V8R 6S4

IN THE UNITED STATES:
Orca Book Publishers
PO Box 468
Custer, WA USA
98240-0468

04 03 02 • 5 4 3 2 1

Solomon's Tree

Written by ANDREA SPALDING
Illustrated by JANET WILSON
Mask and Tsimpshian designs by VICTOR REECE

ORCA BOOK PUBLISHERS

Solomon's Tree

Written by ANDREA SPALDING
Illustrated by JANET WILSON

The cedar trees around Solomon's house were special. They shaded in summer and sheltered in winter and whispered secrets to each other on the breath of the wind.

But the big old maple was very special. This was the tree that shared its secrets with Solomon. Every day Solomon climbed its knobby trunk and curled up in his favorite notch.

"Hello, tree," he whispered and stroked the rough bark.

"Hello, Solomon," the tree rustled back. Its branches cradled his body.

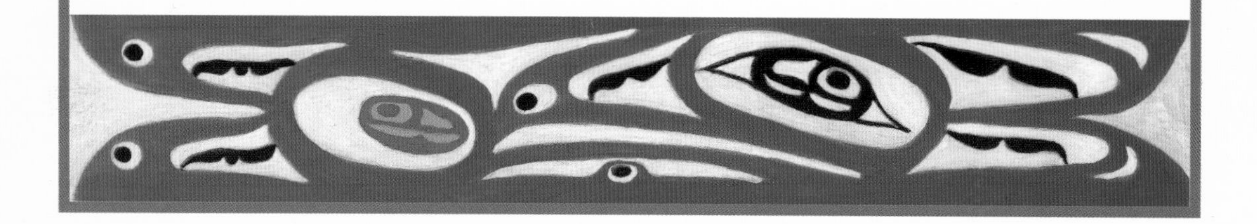

In spring the maple showed him a hummingbird nest. Solomon gazed in astonishment at the fragment of woven lichen clinging to a forked twig and marveled at the tiny eggs, smaller than his little fingernail.

"You mustn't tell," whispered the tree.

"I promise," Solomon whispered back.

In summer the maple showed Solomon where the chrysalis hung, hidden in a crack of bark.

"Watch carefully," whispered the tree.

"I will," Solomon whispered back.

He watched with wonder as the chrysalis cracked open, and bit by bit a brand-new butterfly unfolded its wings and danced away on the breeze.

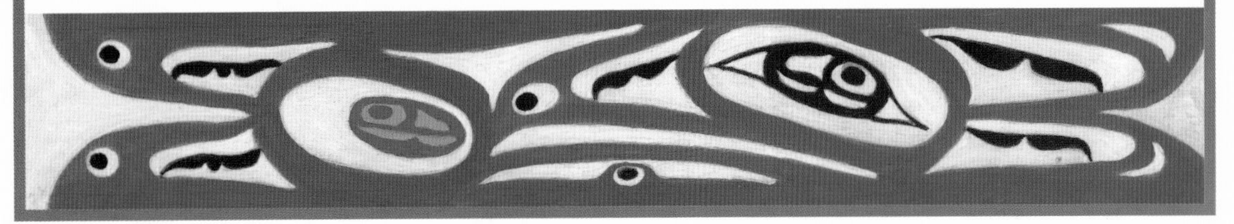

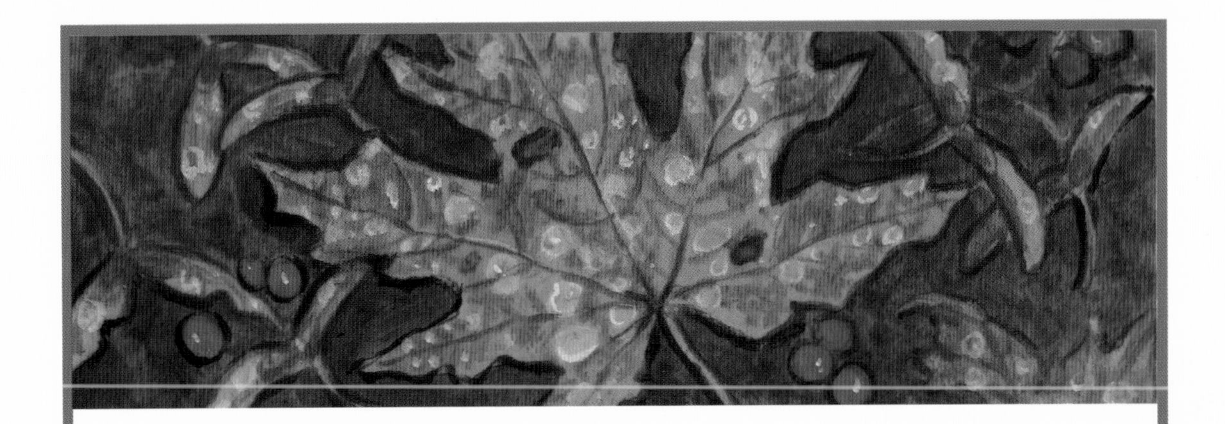

In fall the maple shed its golden leaves and winged seeds and rustled and chuckled as it showered Solomon. Solomon chased the dancing propellers and gathered together piles of leaves.

"Winter's coming," whispered the tree.

"I know," Solomon answered softly from under his leafy blanket.

With the winter came wind and rain. The cedars surrounding Solomon's house tossed their branches and chanted winter songs. The big old maple creaked out lullabies to comfort Solomon's sleep.

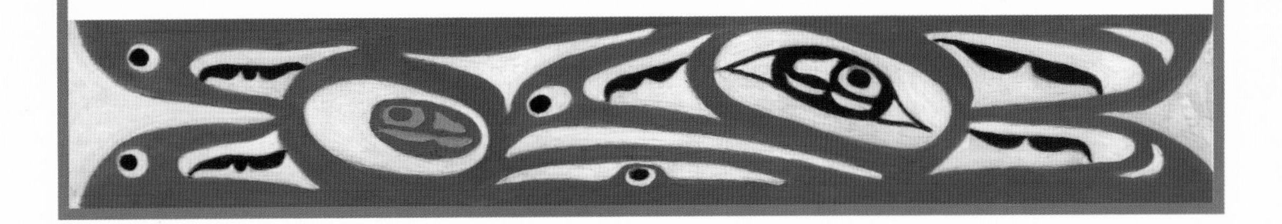

Then came a midwinter storm. The wind howled and shrieked. Inside Solomon's house only the voice of the wind could be heard.

"This storm is too big," said Solomon. "I'm scared." He burrowed under his quilt and pulled the pillow around his ears.

The storm raged for hours, whipping the treetops back and forth and playing a fearsome tug-of-war with their branches. The old maple creaked in protest and writhed and wriggled but couldn't loosen the wind's grip.

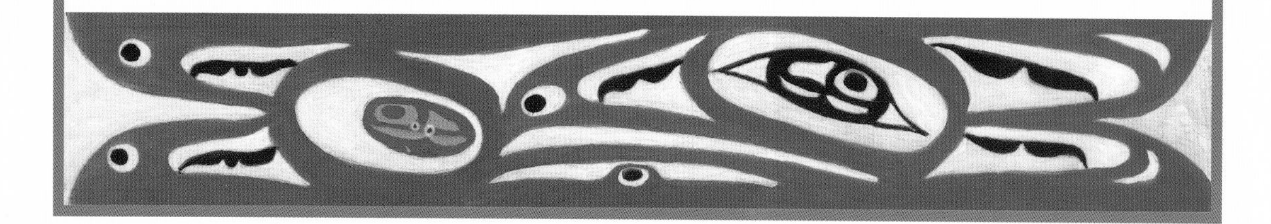

CRAAACK.

The maple gave a last despairing cry, crashed over the woodshed, and fell silent.

"My tree," sobbed Solomon the next morning. He ran through the rain and hugged the fallen trunk. "She was my friend . . . now she's gone . . . and I never said goodbye."

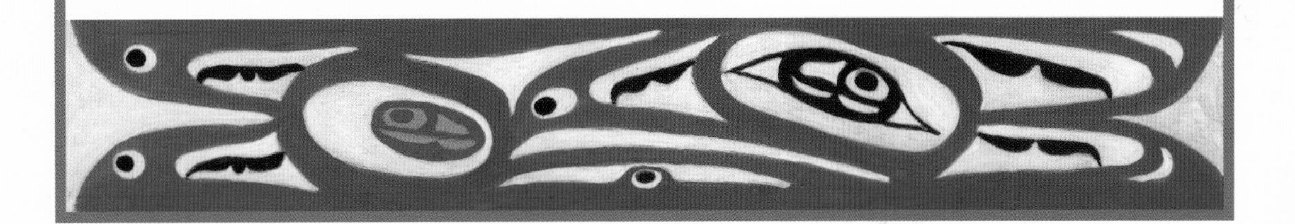

All that day Solomon's family worked. Father used the chain saw to buck up the fallen trunk. Uncle burnt the branches scattered over the driveway and fixed the woodshed. Mother and Solomon stacked the maple logs inside.

Father handed the last log to Solomon and took him to stand in front of Uncle.

"Would you like to see the spirit of your special tree?" Uncle asked.

Solomon nodded.

"Tomorrow we'll start a mask together."

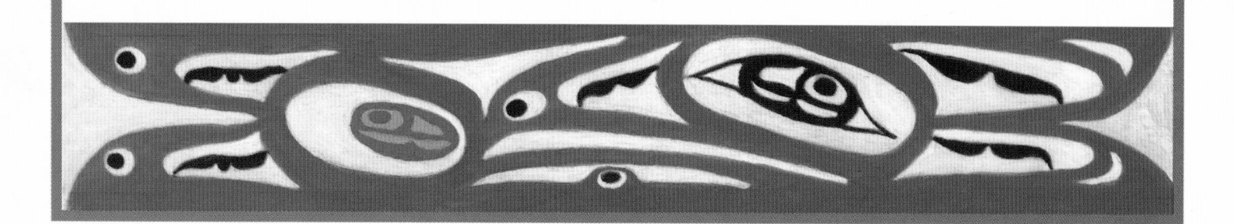

The next day Solomon carried the log to Uncle's workshop. Uncle swung the axe and split it straight down the middle. Solomon clutched half the log to his chest. He closed his eyes and thought about his tree. Uncle picked up his drum and began to dance and sing.

Gwā eee dim haoou,
Here is what I have to say:
Today we begin a carving.
We invite our ancestors to guide us,
To show my nephew the spirit of this special tree.
We honor our ancestors and thank them for their help.

Uncle's voice rang out. His drumming filled the clearing and rose to the sky.

Solomon's voice was small and his feet sad and heavy, but as his Uncle drummed, Solomon grew braver. He sang his own song.

Gwā eee dim haoou,
Here is what I have to say:
Tree, let your spirit guide Uncle's fingers,
Let those fingers show your face,
Let your face help my memory,
Let my memory always honor you.

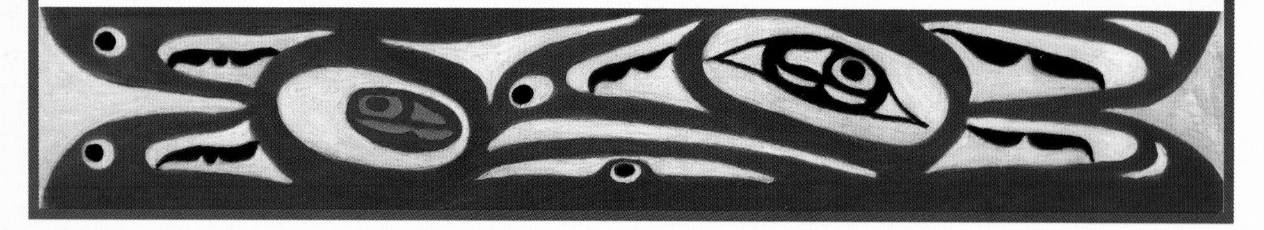

Solomon took the pencil and marked the center ring at each end of his log. Uncle drew a line through the middle and measured on each side.

The chain saw whirred and sawdust flew as Uncle made the first cuts.

Day by day the log transformed.

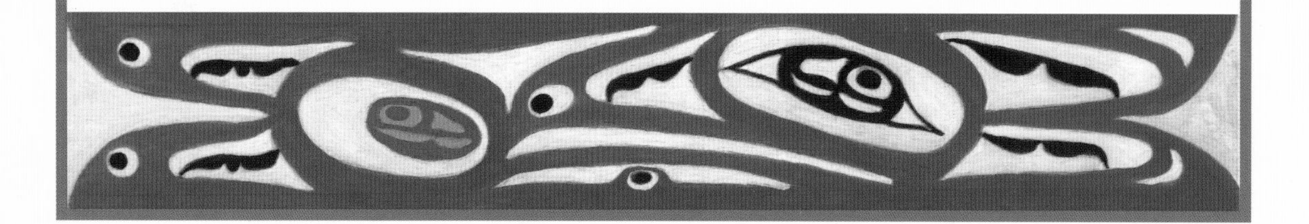

"Tell me about your tree," said Uncle as he planed the angles of the face. "What did you see among the branches?"

Solomon described the hummingbird nest and the antics of the baby birds. Uncle rounded the brow with the adze, chipped the hollows of the eyes, and told the hummingbird story.

"Did your tree smell nice?" asked Uncle as he used the hook knife to carve the nose.

Solomon remembered the sweet spring smell of sap and the pungent fall odor of crushed leaves. Uncle told of fall mushroom gathering in his grandmother's village.

"Did your tree have a voice?" asked Uncle as he showed how to carve the mouth.

Solomon told of whispered secrets and nightly lullabies. Uncle taught Solomon a family song.

"Is my mask finished now?" asked Solomon.

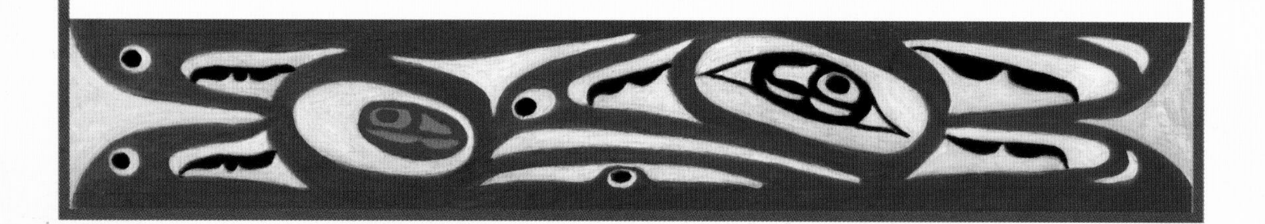

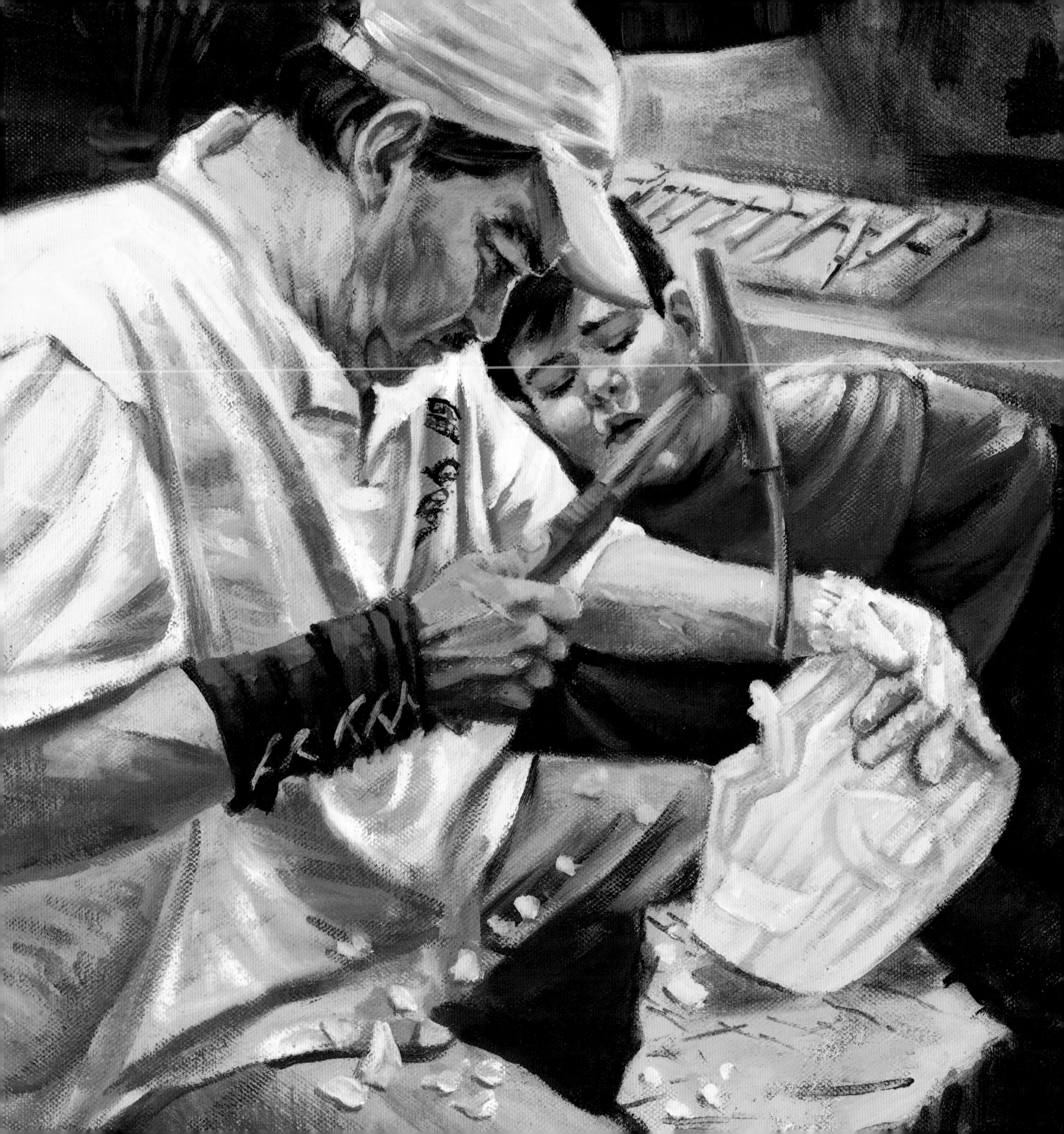

"Not yet. A mask needs to be worn. We must make room for your face. Careful . . . stand back," warned Uncle. He thinned out the back of the mask with the tip of the chain saw. Then he showed Solomon how to hollow the nose and cheeks. Solomon helped scrape and chip. Shavings curled and the mask became thin and beautiful, a face to wear over a face.

Solomon was in charge of drying the mask. He stood on a chair and placed it in the microwave.

"Three times, at three minutes," he said, "with lots of turns."

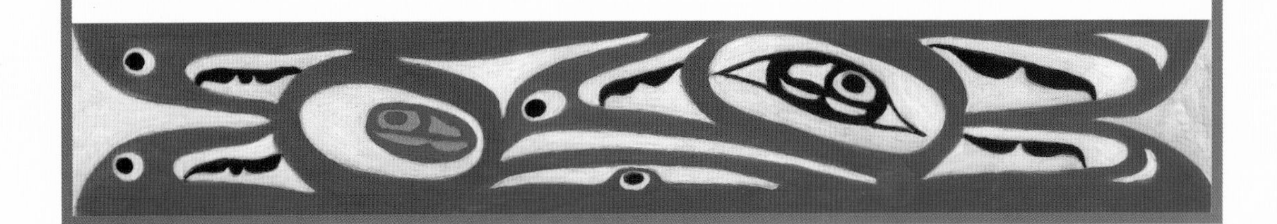

They smoothed and sanded and rubbed and stroked until the face glowed under their fingers and began to look alive.

"Now what?" asked Solomon.

Uncle drew a hummingbird design across the smooth wooden forehead. Next he chose a tiny brush and began to paint. First the beak, then an eye and a face, finally a wing feathering across the brow. Last he painted the outline of the mask's lips and eyeballs, and very, very carefully Solomon filled them in.

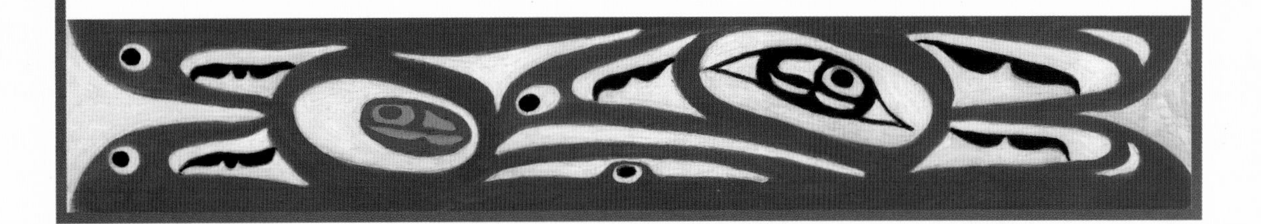

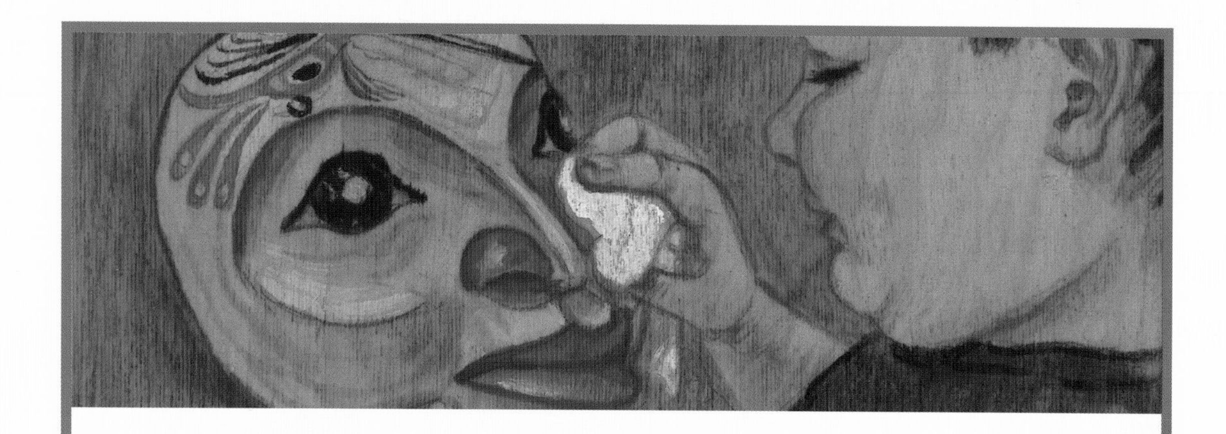

When the paint was dry, Solomon oiled the mask. The wood sprang to life and smiled up at him.

"Hello, tree," whispered Solomon.

"Hello, Solomon," the mask whispered back.

By now a hint of spring was in the air. Solomon and his uncle walked outside into the pale sunshine. The cedars rustled a welcome.

"Mother, Father," shouted Solomon. "Come and see."

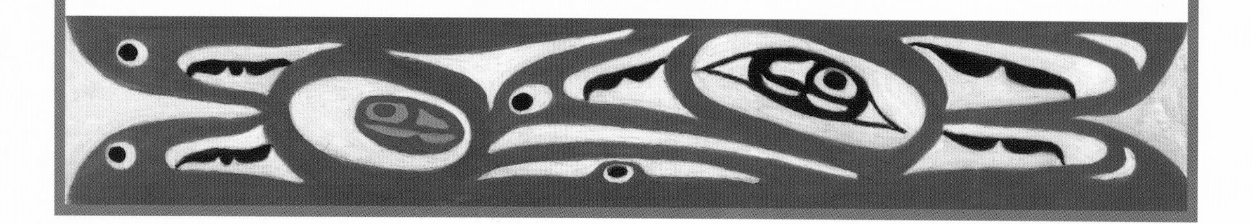

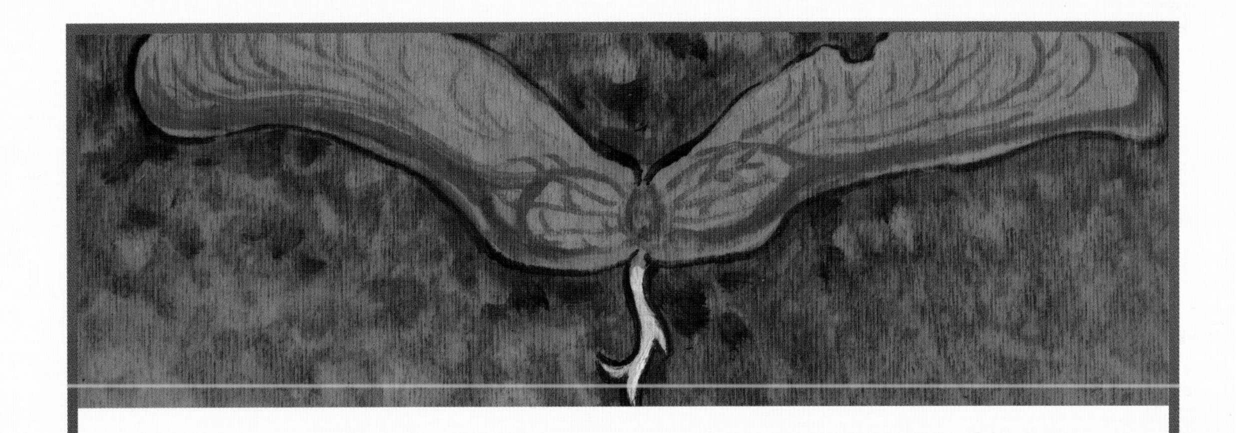

Uncle drummed and everyone sang as Solomon lifted the mask to his face and danced. Beneath their feet the spring sunshine warmed the ground and woke a dormant maple seed. As Solomon danced above, the tip of a root sprouted below and pushed into the loamy earth.

"Ahhh," whispered the cedars to each other. "A new beginning."

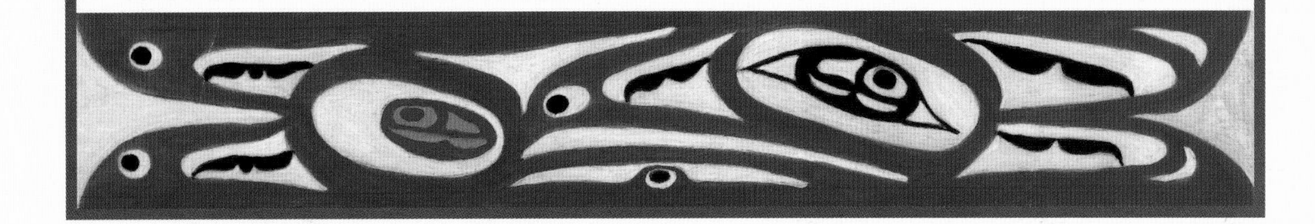

Tsimpshian master-carver Victor Reece created this mask for the story *Solomon's Tree.* Made from alder wood and carved with handmade tools, the face has the wide, high cheeks and deeply carved features typical of the Tsimpshian tradition. The painting across the brow shows a hummingbird in flight.

Victor provided detailed designs from which Janet Wilson painted the strip panels that are located beneath the text on each page and Grandmother Moon, shown on the title page.

For the strip panels, Victor created an elongated raven, for Raven is the trickster and storyteller in Tsimpshian tradition. Each end shows the feathers, with the left-facing beak in the middle and the eye to the right. Raven is looking at her tail. The small bump below the beak is a labret or lip ornament denoting a high-caste woman. Victor calls Andrea Spalding White Raven, so the panel also reflects their friendship.

Grandmother Moon watches over us all. Four spirit canoes for life's journeys frame the bottom portion of her face; symbols of the four directions frame the top portion. The powerful Eagle graces her brow.